THE RUNAWAY SKYSCRAPER

THE RUNAWAY SKYSCRAPER

by Murray Leinster

I

The whole thing started when the clock on the Metropolitan Tower began to run backward. It was not a graceful proceeding. The hands had been moving onward in their customary deliberate fashion, slowly and thoughtfully, but suddenly the people in the offices near the clock's face heard an ominous creaking and groaning. There was a slight, hardly discernible shiver through the tower, and then something gave with a crash. The big hands on the clock began to move backward.

Immediately after the crash all the creaking and groaning ceased, and instead, the usual quiet again hung over everything. One or two of the occupants of the upper offices put their heads out into the halls, but the elevators were running as usual, the lights were burning, and all seemed calm and peaceful. The clerks and stenographers went back to their ledgers and typewriters, the business callers returned to the discussion of their errands, and the ordinary course of business was resumed.

Arthur Chamberlain was dictating a letter to Estelle Woodward, his sole stenographer. When the crash came he paused, listened, and then resumed his task.

It was not a difficult one. Talking to Estelle Woodward was at no time an onerous duty, but it must be admitted that Arthur Chamberlain found it difficult to keep his conversation strictly upon his business.

He was at this time engaged in dictating a letter to his principal creditors, the Gary & Milton Company, explaining that their demand for the immediate payment of the installment then due upon his office furniture was untimely and unjust. A young and budding engineer in New York never has too much money, and when he is young as Arthur Chamberlain was, and as fond of pleasant company, and not too fond of economizing, he is liable to find all demands for payment untimely and he usually considers them unjust as well. Arthur finished dictating the letter and sighed.

"Miss Woodward," he said regretfully, "I am afraid I shall never make a successful man."

Miss Woodward shook her head vaguely. She did not seem to take his remark very seriously, but then, she had learned never to take any of his remarks seriously. She had been puzzled at first by his manner of treating everything with a half-joking pessimism, but now ignored it.

She was interested in her own problems. She had suddenly decided that she was going to be an old maid, and it bothered her. She had discovered that she did not like any one well enough to marry, and she was in her twenty-second year.

She was not a native of New York, and the few young men she had met there she did not care for. She had regretfully decided she was too finicky, too fastidious, but could not seem to help herself. She could not understand their absorption in boxing and baseball and she did not like the way they danced.

She had considered the matter and decided that she would have to reconsider her former opinion of women who did not marry. Heretofore she had thought there must be something the matter with them. Now she believed that she would come to their own estate, and probably for the same reason. She could not fall in love and she wanted to.

She read all the popular novels and thrilled at the love-scenes contained in them, but when any of the young men she knew became in the slightest degree sentimental she found herself bored, and disgusted with herself for being bored. Still, she could not help it, and was struggling to reconcile herself to a life without romance.

She was far too pretty for that, of course, and Arthur Chamberlain often longed to tell her how pretty she really was, but her abstracted air held him at arms' length.

He lay back at ease in his swivel-chair and considered, looking at her with unfeigned pleasure. She did not notice it, for she was so much absorbed in her own thoughts that she rarely noticed anything he said or did when they were not in the line of her duties.

"Miss Woodward," he repeated, "I said I think I'll never make a successful man. Do you know what that means?"

She looked at him mutely, polite inquiry in her eyes.

"It means," he said gravely, "that I'm going broke. Unless something turns up in the next three weeks, or a month at the latest, I'll have to get a job."

"And that means—" she asked.

"All this will go to pot," he explained with a sweeping gesture. "I thought I'd better tell you as much in advance as I could."

"You mean you're going to give up your office—and me?" she asked, a little alarmed.

"Giving up you will be the harder of the two," he said with a smile, "but that's what it means. You'll have no difficulty finding a new place, with three weeks in which to look for one, but I'm sorry."

"I'm sorry, too, Mr. Chamberlain," she said, her brow puckered.

She was not really frightened, because she knew she could get another position, but she became aware of rather more regret than she had expected.

There was silence for a moment.

"Jove!" said Arthur, suddenly. "It's getting dark, isn't it?"

It was. It was growing dark with unusual rapidity. Arthur went to his window, and looked out.

"Funny," he remarked in a moment or two. "Things don't look just right, down there, somehow. There are very few people about."

He watched in growing amazement. Lights came on in the streets below, but none of the buildings lighted up. It grew darker and darker.

"It shouldn't be dark at this hour!" Arthur exclaimed.

Estelle went to the window by his side.

"It looks awfully queer," she agreed. "It must be an eclipse or something."

They heard doors open in the hall outside, and Arthur ran out. The halls were beginning to fill with excited people.

"What on earth's the matter?" asked a worried stenographer.

"Probably an eclipse," replied Arthur. "Only it's odd we didn't read about it in the papers."

He glanced along the corridor. No one else seemed better informed than he, and he went back into his office.

Estelle turned from the window as he appeared.

"The streets are deserted," she said in a puzzled tone. "What's the matter? Did you hear?"

Arthur shook his head and reached for the telephone.

"I'll call up and find out," he said confidently. He held the receiver to his ear. "What the—" he exclaimed. "Listen to this!"

A small-sized roar was coming from the receiver. Arthur hung up and turned a blank face upon Estelle.

"Look!" she said suddenly, and pointed out of the window.

All the city was now lighted up, and such of the signs as they could see were brilliantly illumined. They watched in silence. The streets once more seemed filled with vehicles. They darted along, their headlamps lighting up the roadway brilliantly. There was, however, something strange even about their motion. Arthur and Estelle watched in growing amazement and perplexity.

"Are—are you seeing what I am seeing?" asked Estelle breathlessly. "I see them *going backward!*"

Arthur watched, and collapsed into a chair.

"For the love of Mike!" he exclaimed softly.

▐▌

He was roused by another exclamation from Estelle.

"It's getting light again," she said.

Arthur rose and went eagerly to the window. The darkness was becoming less intense, but in a way Arthur could hardly credit.

Far to the west, over beyond the Jersey hills—easily visible from the height at which Arthur's office was located—a faint light appeared in the sky, grew stronger and then took on a reddish tint. That, in turn, grew deeper, and at last the sun appeared, rising unconcernedly *in the west.*

Arthur gasped. The streets below continued to be thronged with people and motor-cars. The sun was traveling with extraordinary rapidity. It rose overhead, and as if by magic the streets were thronged with people. Every one seemed to be running at top-speed. The few teams they saw moved at a breakneck pace—backward! In spite of the suddenly topsyturvy state of affairs there seemed to be no accidents.

Arthur put his hands to his head.

"Miss Woodward," he said pathetically, "I'm afraid I've gone crazy. Do you see the same things I do?"

Estelle nodded. Her eyes wide open.

"What *is* the matter?" she asked helplessly.

She turned again to the window. The square was almost empty once more. The motor-cars still traveling about the streets were going so swiftly they were hardly visible. Their speed seemed to increase steadily. Soon it was almost impossible to distinguish them, and only a grayish blur marked their paths along Fifth Avenue and Twenty-Third Street.

It grew dusk, and then rapidly dark. As their office was on the western side of the building they could not see that the sun had sunk in the east, but subconsciously they realized that this must be the case.

In silence they watched the panorama grow black except for the street-lamps, remain thus for a time, and then suddenly spring into brilliantly illuminated activity.

Again this lasted for a little while, and the west once more began to glow. The sun rose somewhat more hastily from the Jersey hills and began to soar overhead, but very soon darkness fell again. With hardly an interval the city became illuminated, and then the west grew red once more.

"Apparently," said Arthur, steadying his voice with a conscious effort, "there's been a cataclysm somewhere, the direction of the earth's rotation has been reversed, and its speed immensely increased. It seems to take only about five minutes for a rotation now."

As he spoke darkness fell for the third time. Estelle turned from the window with a white face.

"What's going to happen?" she cried.

"I don't know," answered Arthur. "The scientist fellows tell us if the earth were to spin fast enough the centrifugal force would throw us all off into space. Perhaps that's what's going to happen."

Estelle sank into a chair and stared at him, appalled. There was a sudden explosion behind them. With a start, Estelle jumped to her feet and turned. A little gilt clock over her typewriter-desk lay in fragments. Arthur hastily glanced at his own watch.

"Great bombs and little cannon-balls!" he shouted. "Look at this!"

His watch trembled and quivered in his hand. The hands were going around so swiftly it was impossible to watch the minute-hand, and the hour-hand traveled like the wind.

While they looked, it made two complete revolutions. In one of them the glory of daylight had waxed, waned, and vanished. In the other, darkness reigned except for the glow from the electric light overhead.

There was a sudden tension and catch in the watch. Arthur dropped it instantly. It flew to pieces before it reached the floor.

"If you've got a watch," Arthur ordered swiftly, "stop it this instant!"

Estelle fumbled at her wrist. Arthur tore the watch from her hand and threw open the case. The machinery inside was going so swiftly it was hardly visible; Relentlessly, Arthur jabbed a penholder in the works. There was a sharp click, and the watch was still.

Arthur ran to the window. As he reached it the sun rushed up, day lasted a moment, there was darkness, and then the sun appeared again.

"Miss Woodward!" Arthur ordered suddenly, "look at the ground!"

Estelle glanced down. The next time the sun flashed into view she gasped.

The ground was white with snow!

"What *has* happened?" she demanded, terrified. "Oh, what *has* happened?"

Arthur fumbled at his chin awkwardly, watching the astonishing panorama outside. There was hardly any distinguishing between the times the sun was up and the times it was below now, as the darkness and light followed each other so swiftly the effect was the same as one of the old flickering motion-pictures.

As Arthur watched, this effect became more pronounced. The tall Fifth Avenue Building across the way began to disintegrate. In a moment, it seemed, there was only a skeleton there. Then that vanished, story by story. A great cavity in the earth appeared, and then another building became visible, a smaller, brown-stone, unimpressive structure.

With bulging eyes Arthur stared across the city. Except for the flickering, he could see almost clearly now.

He no longer saw the sun rise and set. There was merely a streak of unpleasantly brilliant light across the sky. Bit by bit, building by building, the city began to disintegrate and become replaced by smaller, dingier buildings. In a little while those began to disappear and leave gaps where they vanished.

Arthur strained his eyes and looked far down-town. He saw a forest of masts and spars along the waterfront for a moment and when he turned his eyes again to the scenery near him it was almost barren of houses, and what few showed were mean, small residences, apparently set in the midst of farms and plantations.

Estelle was sobbing.

"Oh, Mr. Chamberlain," she cried. "What is the matter? What has happened?"

Arthur had lost his fear of what their fate would be in his absorbing interest in what he saw. He was staring out of the window, wide-eyed, lost in the sight before him. At Estelle's cry, however, he reluctantly left the window and patted her shoulder awkwardly.

"I don't know how to explain it," he said uncomfortably, "but it's obvious that my first surmise was all wrong. The speed of the earth's rotation can't have been increased, because if it had to the extent we see, we'd have been thrown off into space long ago. But—have you read anything about the Fourth Dimension?"

Estelle shook her head hopelessly.

"Well, then, have you ever read anything by Wells? The 'Time Machine,' for instance?"

Again she shook her head.

"I don't know how I'm going to say it so you'll understand, but time is just as much a dimension as length and breadth. From what I can judge, I'd say there has been an earthquake, and the ground has settled a little with our building on it, only instead of settling down toward the center of the earth, or side-wise, it's settled in this fourth dimension."

"But what does that mean?" asked Estelle uncomprehendingly.

"If the earth had settled down, we'd have been lower. If it had settled to one side, we'd have been moved one way or another, but as it's settled back in the Fourth Dimension, we're going back in time."

"Then—"

"We're in a runaway skyscraper, bound for some time back before the discovery of America!"

III

It was very still in the office. Except for the flickering outside everything seemed very much as usual. The electric light burned steadily, but Estelle was sobbing with fright and Arthur was trying vainly to console her.

"Have I gone crazy?" she demanded between her sobs.

"Not unless I've gone mad, too," said Arthur soothingly. The excitement had quite a soothing effect upon him. He had ceased to feel afraid, but was simply waiting to see what had happened. "We're way back before the founding of New York now, and still going strong."

"Are you sure that's what has happened?"

"If you'll look outside," he suggested, "you'll see the seasons following each other in reverse order. One moment the snow covers all the ground, then you catch a glimpse of autumn foliage, then summer follows, and next spring."

Estelle glanced out of the window and covered her eyes.

"Not a house," she said despairingly. "Not a building. Nothing, nothing, nothing!"

Arthur slipped, his arm about her and patted hers comfortingly.

"It's all right," he reassured her. "We'll bring up presently, and there'll be. There's nothing to be afraid of."

She rested her head on his shoulder and sobbed hopelessly for a little while longer, but presently quieted. Then, suddenly, realizing that Arthur's arm was about her and that she was crying on his shoulder, she sprang away, blushing crimson.

Arthur walked to the window.

"Look there!" he exclaimed, but it was too late. "I'll swear to it I saw the Half Moon, Hudson's ship," he declared excitedly. "We're way back now, and don't seem to be slacking up, either."

Estelle came to the window by his side. The rapidly changing scene before her made her gasp. It was no longer possible to distinguish night from day.

A wavering streak, moving first to the right and then to the left, showed where the sun flashed across the sky.

"What makes the sun wabble so?" she asked.

"Moving north and south of the equator," Arthur explained casually. "When it's farthest south—to the left—there's always snow on the ground. When it's farthest right it's summer. See how green it is?"

A few moments' observation corroborated his statement.

"I'd say," Arthur remarked reflectively, "that it takes about fifteen seconds for the sun to make the round trip from farthest north to farthest south." He felt his pulse. "Do you know the normal rate of the heart-beat? We can judge time that way. A clock will go all to pieces, of course."

"Why did your watch explode—and the clock?"

"Running forward in time unwinds a clock, doesn't it?" asked Arthur. "It follows, of course, that when you move it backward in time it winds up. When you move it too far back, you wind it so tightly that the spring just breaks to pieces."

He paused a moment, his fingers on his pulse.

"Yes, it takes about fifteen seconds for all the four seasons to pass. That means we're going backward in time about four years a minute. If we go on at this rate another hour we'll be back in the time of the Northmen, and will be able to tell if they did discover America, after all."

"Funny we don't hear any noises," Estelle observed. She had caught some of Arthur's calmness.

"It passes so quickly that though our ears hear it, we don't separate the sounds. If you'll notice, you do hear a sort of humming. It's very high-pitched, though."

Estelle listened, but could hear nothing.

"No matter," said Arthur. "It's probably a little higher than your ears will catch. Lots of people can't hear a bat squeak."

"I never could," said Estelle. "Out in the country, where I come from, other people could hear them, but I couldn't."

They stood a while in silence, watching.

"When are we going to stop?" asked Estelle uneasily. "It seems as if we're going to keep on indefinitely."

"I guess we'll stop all right," Arthur reassured her. "It's obvious that whatever it was, only affected our own building, or we'd see some other one with us. It looks like a fault or a flaw in the rock the building rests on. And that can only give so far."

Estelle was silent for a moment.

"Oh, I can't be sane!" she burst out semihysterically. "This can't be happening!"

"You aren't crazy," said Arthur sharply. "You're sane as I am. Just something queer is happening. Buck up. Say your multiplication tables. Say anything you know. Say something sensible and you'll know you're all right. But don't get frightened now. There'll be plenty to get frightened about later."

The grimness in his tone alarmed Estelle.

"What are you afraid of?" she asked quickly.

"Time enough to worry when it happens," Arthur retorted briefly.

"You—you aren't afraid we'll go back before the beginning of the world, are you?" asked Estelle in sudden access of fright.

Arthur shook his head.

"Tell me," said Estelle more quietly, getting a grip on herself. "I won't mind. But please tell me."

Arthur glanced at her. Her face was pale, but there was more resolution in it than he had expected to find.

"I'll tell you, then," he said reluctantly. "We're going back a little faster than we were, and the flaw seems to be a deeper one than I thought. At the roughest kind of an estimate, we're all of a thousand years before the discovery of America now, and I think nearer three or four. And we're gaining speed all the time. So, though I am as sure as I can be sure of anything that we'll stop this cave-in eventually, I don't know where. It's like a crevasse in the earth opened by an earthquake which may be only a few feet deep, or it may be hundreds of yards, or even a mile or two. We started off smoothly. We're going at a terrific rate. *What will happen when we stop?*"

Estelle caught her breath.

"What?" she asked quietly.

"I don't know," said Arthur in an irritated tone, to cover his apprehension. "How could I know?"

Estelle turned from him to the window again.

"Look!" she said, pointing.

The flickering had begun again. While they stared, hope springing up once more in their hearts, it became more pronounced. Soon they could distinctly see the difference between day and night.

They were slowing up! The white snow on the ground remained there for an appreciable time, autumn lasted quite a while. They could catch the flashes of the sun as it made its revolutions now, instead of its seeming like a ribbon of fire. At last day lasted all of fifteen or twenty minutes.

It grew longer and longer. Then half an hour, then an hour. The sun wavered in midheaven and was still.

Far below them, the watchers in the tower of the skyscraper saw trees swaying and bending in the wind. Though there was not a house or a habitation to be seen and a dense forest covered all of Manhattan Island, such of the world as they could see looked normal. Wherever or rather in whatever epoch of time they were, they had arrived.

IV

Arthur caught at Estelle's arm and the two made a dash for the elevators. Fortunately one was standing still, the door open, on their floor. The elevator-boy had deserted his post and was looking with all the rest of the occupants of the building at the strange landscape that surrounded them.

No sooner had the pair reached the car, however, than the boy came hurrying along the corridor, three or four other people following him also at a run. Without a word the boy rushed inside, the others crowded after him, and the car shot downward, all of the newcomers panting from their sprint.

Theirs was the first car to reach the bottom. They rushed out and to the western door.

Here, where they had been accustomed to see Madison Square spread out before them, a clearing of perhaps half an acre in extent showed itself. Where their eyes instinctively looked for the dark bronze fountain, near which soap-box orators aforetime held sway, they saw a tent, a wigwam of hides and bark gaily painted. And before the wigwam were two or three brown-skinned Indians, utterly petrified with astonishment.

Behind the first wigwam were others, painted like the first with daubs of brightly colored clay. From them, too, Indians issued, and stared in incredulous amazement, their eyes growing wider and wider. When the group of white people confronted the Indians there was a moment's deathlike silence. Then, with a wild yell, the redskins broke and ran, not stopping to gather together their belongings, nor pausing for even a second glance at the weird strangers who invaded their domain.

Arthur took two or three deep breaths of the fresh air and found himself even then comparing its quality with that of the city. Estelle stared about her with unbelieving eyes. She turned and saw the great bulk of the office building behind her, then faced this small clearing with a virgin forest on its farther side.

She found herself trembling from some undefined cause. Arthur glanced at her. He saw the trembling and knew she would have a fit of nerves in a moment if something did not come up demanding instant attention.

"We'd better take a look at this village," he said in an off-hand voice. "We can probably find out how long ago it is from the weapons and so on."

He grasped her arm firmly and led her in the direction of the tents. The other people, left behind, displayed their emotions in different ways. Two or three of them—women—sat frankly down on the steps and indulged in tears of bewilderment, fright and relief in a peculiar combination defying analysis. Two or three of the men swore, in shaken voices.

Meantime, the elevators inside the building were rushing and clanging, and the hall filled with a white-faced mob, desperately anxious to find out what had happened and why. The people poured out of the door and stared about blankly. There was a peculiar expression of doubt on every one of their faces. Each one was asking himself if he were awake, and having proved that by pinches, openly administered, the next query was whether they had gone mad.

Arthur led Estelle cautiously among the tents.

The village contained about a dozen wigwams. Most of them were made of strips of birch-bark, cleverly overlapping each other, the seams cemented with gum. All had hide flaps for doors, and one or two were built almost entirely of hides, sewed together with strips of sinew.

Arthur made only a cursory examination of the village. His principal motive in taking Estelle there was to give her some mental occupation to ward off the reaction from the excitement of the cataclysm.

He looked into one or two of the tents and found merely couches of hides, with minor domestic utensils scattered about. He brought from one tent a bow and quiver of arrows. The workmanship was good, but very evidently the maker had no knowledge of metal tools.

Arthur's acquaintance with archeological subjects was very slight, but he observed that the arrow-heads were chipped, and not rubbed smooth. They were attached to the shafts with strips of gut or tendon.

Arthur was still pursuing his investigation when a sob from Estelle made him stop and look at her.

"Oh, what are we going to do?" she asked tearfully. "What *are* we going to do? Where are we?"

"You mean, *when* are we," Arthur corrected with a grim smile. "I don't know. Way back before the discovery of America, though. You can see in everything in the village that there isn't a trace of European civilization. I suspect that we are several thousand years back. I can't tell, of course, but this pottery makes me think so. See this bowl?"

He pointed to a bowl of red clay lying on the ground before one of the wigwams.

"If you'll look, you'll see that it isn't really pottery at all. It's a basket that was woven of reeds and then smeared with clay to make it fire-resisting. The people who made that didn't know about baking clay to make it stay put. When America was discovered nearly all the tribes knew something about pottery."

"But what are we going to do?" Estelle tearfully insisted.

"We're going to muddle along as well as we can," answered Arthur cheerfully, "until we can get back to where we started from. Maybe the people back in the twentieth century can send a relief party after us. When the skyscraper vanished it must have left a hole of some sort, and it may be possible for them to follow us down."

"If that's so," said Estelle quickly, "why can't we climb up it without waiting for them to come after us?"

Arthur scratched his head. He looked across the clearing at the skyscraper. It seemed to rest very solidly on the ground. He looked up. The sky seemed normal.

"To tell the truth," he admitted, "there doesn't seem to be any hole. I said that more to cheer you up than anything else."

Estelle clenched her hands tightly and took a grip on herself.

"Just tell me the truth," she said quietly. "I was rather foolish, but tell me what you honestly think."

Arthur eyed her keenly.

"In that case," he said reluctantly, "I'll admit we're in a pretty bad fix. I don't know what has happened, how it happened, or anything about it. I'm just going to keep on going until I see a way clear to get out of this mess. There are two thousand of us people, more or less, and among all of us we must be able to find a way out."

Estelle had turned very pale.

"We're in no great danger from Indians," went on Arthur thoughtfully, "or from anything else that I know of—except one thing."

"What is that?" asked Estelle quickly.

Arthur shook his head and led her back toward the skyscraper, which was now thronged with the people from all the floors who had come down to the ground and were standing excitedly about the concourse asking each other what had happened.

23

THE RUNAWAY SKYSCRAPER

Arthur led Estelle to one of the corners.

"Wait for me here," he ordered. "I'm going to talk to this crowd."

He pushed his way through until he could reach the confectionery and news-stand in the main hallway. Here he climbed up on the counter and shouted:

"People, listen to me! I'm going to tell you what's happened!"

In an instant there was dead silence. He found himself the center of a sea of white faces, every one contorted with fear and anxiety.

"To begin with," he said confidently, "there's nothing to be afraid of. We're going to get back to where we started from! I don't know how, yet, but we'll do it. Don't get frightened. Now I'll tell you what's happened."

He rapidly sketched out for them, in words as simple as he could make them, his theory that a flaw in the rock on which the foundations rested had developed and let the skyscraper sink, not downward, but into the Fourth Dimension.

"I'm an engineer," he finished. "What nature can do, we can imitate. Nature let us into this hole. We'll climb out. In the mean time, matters are serious. We needn't be afraid of not getting back. We'll do that. What we've got to fight is—starvation!"

V

"We've got to fight starvation, and we've got to beat it," Arthur continued doggedly. "I'm telling you this right at the outset, because I want you to begin right at the beginning and pitch in to help. We have very little food and a lot of us to eat it. First, I want some volunteers to help with rationing. Next, I want every ounce of food, in this place put under guard where it can be served to those who need it most. Who will help out with this?"

The swift succession of shocks had paralyzed the faculties of most of the people there, but half a dozen moved forward. Among them was a single gray-haired man with an air of accustomed authority. Arthur recognized him as the president of the bank on the ground floor.

"I don't know who you are or if you're right in saying what has happened," said the gray-haired man. "But I see something's got to be done, and—well, for the time being I'll take your word for what that is. Later on we'll thrash this matter out."

Arthur nodded. He bent over and spoke in a low voice to the gray-haired man, who moved away.

"Grayson, Walters, Terhune, Simpson, and Forsythe come here," the gray-haired man called at a doorway.

A number of men began to press dazedly toward him. Arthur resumed his harangue.

"You people—those of you who aren't too dazed to think—are remembering there's a restaurant in the building and no need to starve. You're wrong. There are nearly two thousand of us here. That means six thousand meals a day. We've got to have nearly ten tons of food a day, and we've got to have it at once."

"Hunt?" some one suggested.

THE RUNAWAY SKYSCRAPER

"I saw Indians," some one else shouted. "Can we trade with them?"

"We can hunt and we can trade with the Indians," Arthur admitted, "but we need food by the ton—by the ton, people! The Indians don't store up supplies, and, besides, they're much too scattered to have a surplus for us. But we've got to have food. Now, how many of you know anything about hunting, fishing, trapping, or any possible way of getting food?"

There were a few hands raised—pitifully few. Arthur saw Estelle's hand up.

"Very well," he said. "Those of you who raised your hands then come with me up on the second floor and we'll talk it over. The rest of you try to conquer your fright, and don't go outside for a while. We've got some things to attend to before it will be quite safe for you to venture out. And keep away from the restaurant. There are armed guards over that food. Before we pass it out indiscriminately, we'll see to it there's more for to-morrow and the next day."

He stepped down from the counter and moved toward the stairway. It was not worth while to use the elevator for the ride of only one floor. Estelle managed to join him, and they mounted the steps together.

"Do you think we'll pull through all right?" she asked quietly.

"We've got to!" Arthur told her, setting his chin firmly. "We've simply got to."

The gray-haired president of the bank was waiting for them at the top of the stairs.

"My name is Van Deventer," he said, shaking hands with Arthur, who gave his own name.

"Where shall our emergency council sit?" he asked.

"The bank has a board room right over the safety vault. I dare say we can accommodate everybody there—everybody in the council, anyway."

Arthur followed into the board-room, and the others trooped in after him.

"I'm just assuming temporary leadership," Arthur explained, "because it's imperative some things be done at once. Later on we can talk about electing officials to direct our activities. Right now we need food. How many of you can shoot?"

About a quarter of the hands were raised. Estelle's was among the number.

"And how many are fishermen?"

A few more went up.

"What do the rest of you do?"

There was a chorus of "gardener," "I have a garden in my yard," "I grow peaches in New Jersey," and three men confessed that they raised chickens as a hobby.

"We'll want you gardeners in a little while. Don't go yet. But the most important are huntsmen and fishermen. Have any of you weapons in your offices?"

A number had revolvers, but only one man had a shotgun and shells.

"I was going on my vacation this afternoon straight from the office," he explained, "and have all my vacation tackle."

"Good man!" Arthur exclaimed. "You'll go after the heavy game."

"With a shotgun?" the sportsman asked, aghast.

"If you get close to them a shotgun will do as well as anything, and we can't waste a shell on every bird or rabbit. Those shells of yours are precious. You other fellows will have to turn fishermen for a while. Your pistols are no good for hunting."

27

THE RUNAWAY SKYSCRAPER

"The watchmen at the bank have riot guns," said Van Deventer, "and there are one or two repeating-rifles there. I don't know about ammunition."

"Good! I don't mean about the ammunition, but about the guns. We'll hope for the ammunition. You fishermen get to work to improvise tackle out of anything you can get hold of. Will you do that?"

A series of nods answered his question.

"Now for the gardeners. You people will have to roam through the woods in company with the hunters and locate anything in the way of edibles that grows. Do all of you know what wild plants look like? I mean wild fruits and vegetables that are good to eat."

A few of them nodded, but the majority looked dubious. The consensus of opinion seemed to be that they would try. Arthur seemed a little discouraged.

"I guess you're the man to tell about the restaurant," Van Deventer said quietly. "And as this is the food commission, or something of that sort, everybody here will be better for hearing it. Anyway, everybody will have to know it before night. I took over the restaurant as you suggested, and posted some of the men from the bank that I knew I could trust about the doors. But there was hardly any use in doing it."

"The restaurant stocks up in the afternoon, as most of its business is in the morning and at noon. It only carries a day's stock of foodstuffs, and the—the cataclysm, or whatever it was, came at three o'clock. There is practically nothing in the place. We couldn't make sandwiches for half the women that are caught with us, let alone the men. Everybody will go hungry to-night. There will be no breakfast to-morrow, nor anything to eat until we either make arrangements with the Indians for some supplies or else get food for ourselves."

28

Arthur leaned his jaw on his hand and considered. A slow flush crept over his cheek. He was getting his fighting blood up.

At school, when he began to flush slowly his schoolmates had known the symptom and avoided his wrath. Now he was growing angry with mere circumstances, but it would be none the less unfortunate for those circumstances.

"Well," he said at last deliberately, "we've got to— What's that?"

There was a great creaking and groaning. Suddenly a sort of vibration was felt under foot. The floor began to take on a slight slant.

"Great Heaven!" some one cried. "The building's turning over and we'll be buried in the ruins!"

The tilt of the floor became more pronounced. An empty chair slid to one end of the room. There was a crash.

VI

Arthur woke to find some one tugging at his shoulders, trying to drag him from beneath the heavy table, which had wedged itself across his feet and pinned him fast, while a flying chair had struck him on the head and knocked him unconscious.

"Oh, come and help," Estelle's voice was calling deliberately. "Somebody come and help! He's caught in here!"

She was sobbing in a combination of panic and some unknown emotion.

"Help me, please!" she gasped, then her voice broke despondently, but she never ceased to tug ineffectually at Chamberlain, trying to drag him out of the mass of wreckage.

Arthur moved a little, dazedly.

"Are you alive?" she called anxiously. "Are you alive? Hurry, oh, hurry and wriggle out. The building's falling to pieces!"

"I'm all right," Arthur said weakly. "You get out before it all comes down."

"I won't leave you," she declared "Where are you caught? Are you badly hurt? Hurry, please hurry!"

Arthur stirred, but could not loosen his feet. He half-rolled over, and the table moved as if it had been precariously balanced, and slid heavily to one side. With Estelle still tugging at him, he managed to get to his feet on the slanting floor and stared about him.

Arthur continued to stare about.

"No danger," he said weakly. "Just the floor of the one room gave way. The aftermath of the rock-flaw."

He made his way across the splintered flooring and piled-up chairs.

"We're on top of the safe-deposit vault," he said. "That's why we didn't fall all the way to the floor below. I wonder how we're going to get down?"

Estelle followed him, still frightened for fear of the building falling upon them. Some of the long floor-boards stretched over the edge of the vault and rested on a tall, bronze grating that protected the approach to the massive strong-box. Arthur tested them with his foot.

"They seem to be pretty solid," he said tentatively.

His strength was coming back to him every moment. He had been no more than stunned. He walked out on the planking to the bronze grating and turned.

"If you don't get dizzy, you might come on," he said. "We can swing down the grille here to the floor."

Estelle followed gingerly and in a moment they were safely below. The corridor was quite empty.

"When the crash came," Estelle explained, her voice shaking with the reaction from her fear of a moment ago, "every one thought the building was coming to pieces, and ran out. I'm afraid they've all run away."

"They'll be back in a little while," Arthur said quietly.

They went along the big marble corridor to the same western door, out of which they had first gone to see the Indian village. As they emerged into the sunlight they met a few of the people who had already recovered from their panic and were returning.

A crowd of respectable size gathered in a few moments, all still pale and shaken, but coming back to the building which was their refuge. Arthur leaned wearily against the cold stone. It seemed to vibrate under his touch. He turned quickly to Estelle.

"Feel this," he exclaimed.

She did so.

"I've been wondering what that rumble was," she said. "I've been hearing it ever since we landed here, but didn't understand where it came from."

"You hear a rumble?" Arthur asked, puzzled. "I can't hear anything."

"It isn't as loud as it was, but I hear it," Estelle insisted. "It's very deep, like the lowest possible bass note of an organ."

"You couldn't hear the shrill whistle when we were coming here," Arthur exclaimed suddenly, "and you can't hear the squeak of a bat. Of course your ears are pitched lower than usual, and you can hear sounds that are lower than I can hear. Listen carefully. Does it sound in the least like a liquid rushing through somewhere?"

"Y-yes," said Estelle hesitatingly. "Somehow, I don't quite understand how, it gives me the impression of a tidal flow or something of that sort."

Arthur rushed indoors. When Estelle followed him she found him excitedly examining the marble floor about the base of the vault.

"It's cracked," he said excitedly. "It's cracked! The vault rose all of an inch!"

Estelle looked and saw the cracks.

"What does that mean?"

"It means we're going to get back where we belong," Arthur cried jubilantly. "It means I'm on the track of the whole trouble. It means everything's going to be all right."

He prowled about the vault exultantly, noting exactly how the cracks in the flooring ran and seeing in each a corroboration of his theory.

"I'll have to make some inspections in the cellar," he went on happily, "but I'm nearly sure I'm on the right track and can figure out a corrective."

"How soon can we hope to start back?" asked Estelle eagerly.

Arthur hesitated, then a great deal of the excitement ebbed from his face, leaving it rather worried and stern.

"It may be a month, or two months, or a year," he answered gravely. "I don't know. If the first thing I try will work, it won't be long. If we have to experiment, I daren't guess how long we may be. But"—his chin set firmly—"we're going to get back."

Estelle looked at him speculatively. Her own expression grew a little worried, too.

"But in a month," she said dubiously, "we—there is hardly any hope of our finding food for two thousand people for a month, is there?"

"We've got to," Arthur declared. "We can't hope to get that much food from the Indians. It will be days before they'll dare to come back to their village, if they ever come. It will be weeks before we can hope to have them earnestly at work to feed us, and that's leaving aside the question of how we'll communicate with them, and how we'll manage to trade with them. Frankly, I think everybody is going to have to draw his belt tight before we get through—if we do. Some of us will get along, anyway."

Estelle's eyes opened wide as the meaning of his last sentence penetrated her mind.

"You mean—that all of us won't—"

"I'm going to take care of you," Arthur said gravely, "but there are liable to be lively doings around here when people begin to realize they're really in a tight fix for food. I'm going to get Van Deventer to help me organize a police band to enforce martial law. We mustn't have any disorder, that's certain, and I don't trust a city-bred man in a pinch unless I know him."

THE RUNAWAY SKYSCRAPER

He stooped and picked up a revolver from the floor, left there by one of the bank watchmen when he fled, in the belief that the building was falling.

VII

Arthur stood at the window of his office and stared out toward the west. The sun was setting, but upon what a scene!

Where, from this same window Arthur had seen the sun setting behind the Jersey hills, all edged with the angular roofs of factories, with their chimneys emitting columns of smoke, he now saw the same sun sinking redly behind a mass of luxuriant foliage. And where he was accustomed to look upon the tops of high buildings—each entitled to the name of "skyscraper"—he now saw miles and miles of waving green branches.

The wide Hudson flowed on placidly, all unruffled by the arrival of this strange monument upon its shores—the same Hudson Arthur knew as a busy thoroughfare of puffing steamers and chugging launches. Two or three small streams wandered unconcernedly across the land that Arthur had known as the most closely built-up territory on earth. And far, far below him—Arthur had to lean well out of his window to see it—stood a collection of tiny wigwams. Those small bark structures represented the original metropolis of New York.

His telephone rang. Van Deventer was on the wire. The exchange in the building was still working. Van Deventer wanted Arthur to come down to his private office. There were still a great many things to be settled—the arrangements for commandeering offices for sleeping quarters for the women, and numberless other details. The men who seemed to have best kept their heads were gathering there to settle upon a course of action.

Arthur glanced out of the window again before going to the elevator. He saw a curiously compact dark cloud moving swiftly across the sky to the west.

"Miss Woodward," he said sharply, "What is that?"

Estelle came to the window and looked.

"They are birds," she told him. "Birds flying in a group. I've often seen them in the country, though never as many as that."

"How do you catch birds?" Arthur asked her. "I know about shooting them, and so on, but we haven't guns enough to count. Could we catch them in traps, do you think?"

"I wouldn't be surprised," said Estelle thoughtfully. "But it would be hard to catch many."

"Come down-stairs," directed Arthur. "You know as much as any of the men here, and more than most, apparently. We're going to make you show us how to catch things."

Estelle smiled, a trifle wanly. Arthur led the way to the elevator. In the car he noticed that she looked distressed.

"What's the matter?" he asked. "You aren't really frightened, are you?"

"No," she answered shakily, "but—I'm rather upset about this thing. It's so—so terrible, somehow, to be back here, thousands of miles, or years, away from all one's friends and everybody."

"Please"—Arthur smiled encouragingly at her—"please count me your friend, won't you?"

She nodded, but blinked back some tears. Arthur would have tried to hearten her further, but the elevator stopped at their floor. They walked into the room where the meeting of cool heads was to take place.

No more than a dozen men were in there talking earnestly but dispiritedly. When Arthur and Estelle entered Van Deventer came over to greet them.

"We've got to do something," he said in a low voice. "A wave of homesickness has swept over the whole place. Look at those men.

Every one is thinking about his family and contrasting his cozy fireside with all that wilderness outside."

"You don't seem to be worried," Arthur observed with a smile.

Van Deventer's eyes twinkled.

"I'm a bachelor," he said cheerfully, "and I live in a hotel. I've been longing for a chance to see some real excitement for thirty years. Business has kept me from it up to now, but I'm enjoying myself hugely."

Estelle looked at the group of dispirited men.

"We'll simply have to do something," she said with a shaky smile. "I feel just as they do. This morning I hated the thought of having to go back to my boarding-house to-night, but right now I feel as if the odor of cabbage in the hallway would seem like heaven."

Arthur led the way to the flat-topped desk in the middle of the room.

"Let's settle a few of the more important matters," he said in a businesslike tone. "None of us has any authority to act for the rest of the people in the tower, but so many of us are in a state of blue funk that those who are here must have charge for a while. Anybody any suggestions?"

"Housing," answered Van Deventer promptly. "I suggest that we draft a gang of men to haul all the upholstered settees and rugs that are to be found to one floor, for the women to sleep on."

"M—m. Yes. That's a good idea. Anybody a better plan?"

No one spoke. They all still looked much too homesick to take any great interest in anything, but they began to listen more or less half-heartedly.

"I've been thinking about coal," said Arthur. "There's undoubtedly a supply in the basement, but I wonder if it wouldn't be well to cut the lights off most of the floors, only lighting up the ones we're using."

"That might be a good idea later," Estelle said quietly, "but light is cheering, somehow, and every one feels so blue that I wouldn't do it to-night. To-morrow they'll begin to get up their resolution again, and you can ask them to do things."

"If we're going to starve to death," one of the other men said gloomily, "we might as well have plenty of light to do it by."

"We aren't going to starve to death," retorted Arthur sharply. "Just before I came down I saw a great cloud of birds, greater than I had ever seen before. When we get at those birds—"

"When," echoed the gloomy one.

"They were pigeons," Estelle explained. "They shouldn't be hard to snare or trap."

"I usually have my dinner before now," the gloomy one protested, "and I'm told I won't get anything to-night."

The other men began to straighten their shoulders. The peevishness of one of their number seemed to bring out their latent courage.

"Well, we've got to stand it for the present," one of them said almost philosophically. "What I'm most anxious about is getting back. Have we any chance?"

Arthur nodded emphatically.

"I think so. I have a sort of idea as to the cause of our sinking into the Fourth Dimension, and when that is verified, a corrective can be looked for and applied."

"How long will that take?"

"Can't say," Arthur replied frankly. "I don't know what tools, what materials, or what workmen we have, and what's rather more to the point, I don't even know what work will have to be done. The pressing problem is food."

"Oh, bother the food," some one protested impatiently. "I don't care about myself. I can go hungry to-night. I want to get back to my family."

"That's all that really matters," a chorus of voices echoed.

"We'd better not bother about anything else unless we find we can't get back. Concentrate on getting back," one man stated more explicitly.

"Look here," said Arthur incisively. "You've a family, and so have a great many of the others in the tower, but your family and everybody else's family has got to wait. As an inside limit, we can hope to begin to work on the problem of getting back when we're sure there's nothing else going to happen. I tell you quite honestly that I think I know what is the direct cause of this catastrophe. And I'll tell you even more honestly that I think I'm the only man among us who can put this tower back where it started from. And I'll tell you most honestly of all that any attempt to meddle at this present time with the forces that let us down here will result in a catastrophe considerably greater than the one that happened to-day."

"Well, if you're sure—" some one began reluctantly.

"I am so sure that I'm going to keep to myself the knowledge of what will start those forces to work again," Arthur said quietly. "I don't want any impatient meddling. If we start them too soon God only knows what will happen."

VIII

Van Deventer was eying Arthur Chamberlain keenly.

"It isn't a question of your wanting pay in exchange for your services in putting us back, is it?" he asked coolly.

Arthur turned and faced him. His face began to flush slowly. Van Deventer put up one hand.

"I beg your pardon. I see."

"We aren't settling the things we came here for," Estelle interrupted.

She had noted the threat of friction and hastened to put in a diversion. Arthur relaxed.

"I think that as a beginning," he suggested, "we'd better get sleeping arrangements completed. We can get everybody together somewhere, I dare say, and then secure volunteers for the work."

"Right." Van Deventer was anxious to make amends for his blunder of a moment before. "Shall I send the bank watchmen to go on each floor in turn and ask everybody to come down-stairs?"

"You might start them," Arthur said. "It will take a long time for every one to assemble."

Van Deventer spoke into the telephone on his desk. In a moment he hung up the receiver.

"They're on their way," he said.

Arthur was frowning to himself and scribbling in a note-book.

"Of course," he announced abstractedly, "the pressing problem is food. We've quite a number of fishermen, and a few hunters. We've got to have a lot of food at once, and everything considered, I think we'd better count on the fishermen. At sunrise we'd better have some people begin to dig bait and wake our anglers. They'd better make their tackle to-night, don't you think?"

40

There was a general nod.

"We'll announce that, then. The fishermen will go to the river under guard of the men we have who can shoot. I think what Indians there are will be much too frightened to try to ambush any of us, but we'd better be on the safe side. They'll keep together and fish at nearly the same spot, with our hunters patrolling the woods behind them, taking pot-shots at game, if they see any. The fishermen should make more or less of a success, I think. The Indians weren't extensive fishers that I ever heard of, and the river ought fairly to swarm with fish."

He closed his note-book.

"How many weapons can we count on altogether?" Arthur asked Van Deventer.

"In the bank, about a dozen riot-guns and half a dozen repeating rifles. Elsewhere I don't know. Forty or fifty men said they had revolvers, though."

"We'll give revolvers to the men who go with the fishermen. The Indians haven't heard firearms and will run at the report, even if they dare attack our men."

"We can send out the gun-armed men as hunters," some one suggested, "and send gardeners with them to look for vegetables and such things."

"We'll have to take a sort of census, really," Arthur suggested, "finding what every one can do and getting him to do it."

"I never planned anything like this before," Van Deventer remarked, "and I never thought I should, but this is much more fun than running a bank."

Arthur smiled.

"Let's go and have our meeting," he said cheerfully.

THE RUNAWAY SKYSCRAPER

But the meeting was a gloomy and despairing affair. Nearly every one had watched the sun set upon a strange, wild landscape. Hardly an individual among the whole two thousand of them had ever been out of sight of a house before in his or her life. To look out at a vast, untouched wilderness where hitherto they had seen the most highly civilized city on the globe would have been startling and depressing enough in itself, but to know that they were alone in a whole continent of savages and that there was not, indeed, in all the world a single community of people they could greet as brothers was terrifying.

Few of them thought so far, but there was actually—if Arthur's estimate of several thousand years' drop back through time was correct—there was actually no other group of English-speaking people in the world. The English language was yet to be invented. Even Rome, the synonym for antiquity of culture, might still be an obscure village inhabited by a band of tatterdemalions under the leadership of an upstart Romulus.

Soft in body as these people were, city-bred and unaccustomed to face other than the most conventionalized emergencies of life, they were terrified. Hardly one of them had even gone without a meal in all his life. To have the prospect of having to earn their food, not by the manipulation of figures in a book, or by expert juggling of profits and prices, but by literal wresting of that food from its source in the earth or stream was a really terrifying thing for them.

In addition, every one of them was bound to the life of modern times by a hundred ties. Many of them had families, a thousand years away. All had interests, engrossing interests, in modern New York.

One young man felt an anxiety that was really ludicrous because he had promised to take his sweetheart to the theater that night, and if he did not come she would be very angry. Another was to have been married in a week. Some of the people were, like Van Deventer and Arthur, so situated that they could view the episode as an adventure, or, like Estelle, who had no immediate fear because all her family was provided for without her help and lived far from New York, so they would not learn of the catastrophe for some time. Many, however, felt instant and pressing fear for the families whose expenses ran always so close to their incomes that the disappearance of the breadwinner for a week would mean actual want or debt. There are very many such families in New York.

The people, therefore, that gathered hopelessly at the call of Van Deventer's watchmen were dazed and spiritless. Their excitement after Arthur's first attempt to explain the situation to them had evaporated. They were no longer keyed up to a high pitch by the startling thing that had happened to them.

Nevertheless, although only half comprehending what had actually occurred, they began to realize what that occurrence meant. No matter where they might go over the whole face of the globe, they would always be aliens and strangers. If they had been carried away to some unknown shore, some wilderness far from their own land, they might have thought of building ships to return to their homes. They had seen New York vanish before their eyes, however. They had seen their civilization disappear while they watched.

They were in a barbarous world. There was not, for example, a single sulfur match on the whole earth except those in the runaway skyscraper.

IX

Arthur and Van Deventer, in turn with the others of the cooler heads, thundered at the apathetic people, trying to waken them to the necessity for work. They showered promises of inevitable return to modern times, they pledged their honor to the belief that a way would ultimately be found by which they would all yet find themselves safely back home again.

The people, however, had seen New York disintegrate, and Arthur's explanation sounded like some wild dream of an imaginative novelist. Not one person in all the gathering could actually realize that his home might yet be waiting for him, though at the same time he felt a pathetic anxiety for the welfare of its inmates.

Every one was in a turmoil of contradictory beliefs. On the one hand they knew that all of New York could not be actually destroyed and replaced by a splendid forest in the space of a few hours, so the accident or catastrophe must have occurred to those in the tower, and on the other hand, they had seen all of New York vanish by bits and fragments, to be replaced by a smaller and dingier town, had beheld that replaced in turn, and at last had landed in the midst of this forest.

Every one, too, began to feel am unusual and uncomfortable sensation of hunger. It was a mild discomfort as yet, but few of them had experienced it before without an immediate prospect of assuaging the craving, and the knowledge that there was no food to be had somehow increased the desire for it. They were really in a pitiful state.

Van Deventer spoke encouragingly, and then asked for volunteers for immediate work. There was hardly any response. Every one seemed sunk in despondency. Arthur then began to talk straight from the shoulder and succeeded in rousing them a little, but every one was still rather too frightened to realize that work could help at all.

In desperation the dozen or so men who had gathered in Van Deventer's office went about among the gathering and simply selected men at random, ordering them to follow and begin work. This began to awaken the crowd, but they wakened to fear rather than resolution. They were city-bred, and unaccustomed to face the unusual or the alarming.

Arthur noted the new restlessness, but attributed it to growing uneasiness rather than selfish panic. He was rather pleased that they were outgrowing their apathy. When the meeting had come to an end he felt satisfied that by morning the latent resolution among the people would have crystallized and they would be ready to work earnestly and intelligently on whatever tasks they were directed to undertake.

He returned to the ground floor of the building feeling much more hopeful than before. Two thousand people all earnestly working for one end are hard to down even when faced with such a task as confronted the inhabitants of the runaway skyscraper. Even if they were never able to return to modern times they would still be able to form a community that might do much to hasten the development of civilization in other parts of the world.

His hope received a rude shock when he reached the great hallway on the lower floor. There was a fruit and confectionery stand here, and as Arthur arrived at the spot, he saw a surging mass of men about it. The keeper of the stand looked frightened, but was selling off his stock as fast as he could make change. Arthur forced his way to the counter.

"Here," he said sharply to the keeper of the stand, "stop selling this stuff. It's got to be held until we can dole it out where it's needed."

"I—I can't help myself," the keeper said. "They're takin' it anyway."

"Get back there," Arthur cried to the crowd. "Do you call this decent, trying to get more than your share of this stuff? You'll get your portion to-morrow. It is going to be divided up."

"Go to hell!" some one panted. "You c'n starve if you want to, but I'm goin' to look out f'r myself."

The men were not really starving, but had been put into a panic by the plain speeches of Arthur and his helpers, and were seizing what edibles they could lay hands upon in preparation for the hunger they had been warned to expect.

Arthur pushed against the mob, trying to thrust them away from the counter, but his very effort intensified their panic. There was a quick surge and a crash. The glass front of the showcase broke in.

In a flash of rage Arthur struck out viciously. The crowd paid not the slightest attention to him, however. Every man was too panic-stricken, and too intent on getting some of this food before it was all gone to bother with him.

Arthur was simply crushed back by the bodies of the forty or fifty men. In a moment he found himself alone amid the wreckage of the stand, with the keeper wringing his hands over the remnants of his goods.

Van Deventer ran down the stairs.

"What's the matter?" he demanded as he saw Arthur nursing a bleeding hand cut on the broken glass of the showcase.

"Bolsheviki!" answered Arthur with a grim smile. "We woke up some of the crowd too successfully. They got panic-stricken and started to buy out this stuff here. I tried to stop them, and you see what happened. We'd better look to the restaurant, though I doubt if they'll try anything else just now."

He followed Van Deventer up to the restaurant floor. There were picked men before the door, but just as Arthur and the bank president appeared two or three white-faced men went up to the guards and started low-voiced conversations.

Arthur reached the spot in time to forestall bribery.

Arthur collared one man, Van Deventer another, and in a moment the two were sent reeling down the hallway.

"Some fools have got panic-stricken!" Van Deventer explained to the men before the doors in a casual voice, though he was breathing heavily from the unaccustomed exertion. "They've smashed up the fruit-stand on the ground floor and stolen the contents. It's nothing but blue funk! Only, if any of them start to gather around here, hit them first and talk it over afterward. You'll do that?"

"We will!" the men said heartily.

"Shall we use our guns?" asked another hopefully.

Van Deventer grinned.

"No," he replied, "we haven't any excuse for that yet. But you might shoot at the ceiling, if they get excited. They're just frightened!"

He took Arthur's arm, and the two walked toward the stairway again.

"Chamberlain," he said happily, "tell me why I've never had as much fun as this before!"

Arthur smiled a bit wearily.

"I'm glad you're enjoying yourself!" he said. "I'm not. I'm going outside and walk around. I want to see if any cracks have appeared in the earth anywhere. It's dark, and I'll borrow a lantern down in the fire-room, but I want to find out if there are any more developments in the condition of the building."

X

Despite his preoccupation with his errand, which was to find if there were other signs of the continued activity of the strange forces that had lowered the tower through the Fourth Dimension into the dim and unrecorded years of aboriginal America, Arthur could not escape the fascination of the sight that met his eyes. A bright moon shone overhead and silvered the white sides of the tower, while the brightly-lighted windows of the offices within glittered like jewels set into the shining shaft.

From his position on the ground he looked into the dimness of the forest on all sides. Black obscurity had gathered beneath the dark masses of moonlit foliage. The tiny birch-bark teepees of the now deserted Indian village glowed palely. Above, the stars looked calmly down at the accusing finger of the tower pointing upward, as if in reproach at their indifference to the savagery that reigned over the whole earth.

Like a fairy tower of jewels the building rose. Alone among a wilderness of trees and streams it towered in a strange beauty: moonlit to silver, lighted from within to a mass of brilliant gems, it stood serenely still.

Arthur, carrying his futile lantern about its base, felt his own insignificance as never before. He wondered what the Indians must think. He knew there must be hundreds of eyes fixed upon the strange sight—fixed in awe-stricken terror or superstitious reverence upon this unearthly visitor to their hunting grounds.

A tiny figure, dwarfed by the building whose base he skirted, Arthur moved slowly about the vast pile. The earth seemed not to have been affected by the vast weight of the tower.

Arthur knew, however, that long concrete piles reached far down to bedrock. It was these piles that had sunk into the Fourth Dimension, carrying the building with them.

Arthur had followed the plans with great interest when the Metropolitan was constructed. It was an engineering feat, and in the engineering periodicals, whose study was a part of Arthur's business, great space had been given to the building and the methods of its construction.

While examining the earth carefully he went over his theory of the cause for the catastrophe. The whole structure must have sunk at the same time, or it, too, would have disintegrated, as the other buildings had appeared to disintegrate. Mentally, Arthur likened the submergence of the tower in the oceans of time to an elevator sinking past the different floors of an office building. All about the building the other sky-scrapers of New York had seemed to vanish. In an elevator, the floors one passes seem to rise upward.

Carrying out the analogy to its logical end, Arthur reasoned that the building itself had no more cause to disintegrate, as the buildings it passed seemed to disintegrate, than the elevator in the office building would have cause to rise because its surroundings seemed to rise.

Within the building, he knew, there were strange stirrings of emotions. Queer currents of panic were running about, throwing the people to and fro as leaves are thrown about by a current of wind. Yet, underneath all those undercurrents of fear, was a rapidly growing resolution, strengthened by an increasing knowledge of the need to work.

Men were busy even then shifting all possible comfortable furniture to a single story for the women in the building to occupy. The men would sleep on the floor for the present. Beds of boughs could be improvised on the morrow. At sunrise on the following morning many men would go to the streams to fish, guarded by other men. All would be frightened, no doubt, but there would be a grim resolution underneath the fear. Other men would wander about to hunt.

There was little likelihood of Indians approaching for some days, at least, but when they did come Arthur meant to avoid hostilities by all possible means. The Indians would be fearful of their strange visitors, and it should not be difficult to convince them that friendliness was safest, even if they displayed unfriendly desires.

The pressing problem was food. There were two thousand people in the building, soft-bodied and city-bred. They were unaccustomed to hardship, and could not endure what more primitive people would hardly have noticed.

They must be fed, but first they must be taught to feed themselves. The fishermen would help, but Arthur could only hope that they would prove equal to the occasion. He did not know what to expect from them. From the hunters he expected but little. The Indians were wary hunters, and game would be shy if not scarce.

The great cloud of birds he had seen at sunset was a hopeful sign. Arthur vaguely remembered stories of great flocks of wood-pigeons which had been exterminated, as the buffalo was exterminated. As he considered the remembrance became more clear.

They had flown in huge flocks which nearly darkened the sky. As late as the forties of the nineteenth century they had been an important article of food, and had glutted the market at certain seasons of the year.

Estelle had said the birds he had seen at sunset were pigeons. Perhaps this was one of the great flocks. If it were really so, the food problem would be much lessened, provided a way could be found to secure them. The ammunition in the tower was very limited, and a shell could not be found for every bird that was needed, nor even for every three or four. Great traps must be devised, or bird-lime might possibly be produced. Arthur made a mental note to ask Estelle if she knew anything of bird-lime.

A vague, humming roar, altering in pitch, came to his ears. He listened for some time before he identified it as the sound of the wind playing upon the irregular surfaces of the tower. In the city the sound was drowned by the multitude of other noises, but here Arthur could hear it plainly.

He listened a moment, and became surprised at the number of night noises he could hear. In New York he had closed his ears to incidental sounds from sheer self-protection. Somewhere he heard the ripple of a little spring. As the idea of a spring came into his mind, he remembered Estelle's description of the deep-toned roar she had heard.

He put his hand on the cold stone of the building. There was still a vibrant quivering of the rock. It was weaker than before, but was still noticeable.

He drew back from the rock and looked up into the sky. It seemed to blaze with stars, far more stars than Arthur had ever seen in the city, and more than he had dreamed existed.

As he looked, however, a cloud seemed to film a portion of the heavens. The stars still showed through it, but they twinkled in a peculiar fashion that Arthur could not understand.

He watched in growing perplexity. The cloud moved very swiftly. Thin as it seemed to be, it should have been silvery from the moonlight, but the sky was noticeably darker where it moved. It advanced toward the tower and seemed to obscure the upper portion. A confused motion became visible among its parts. Wisps of it whirled away from the brilliantly lighted tower, and then returned swiftly toward it.

Arthur heard a faint tinkle, then a musical scraping, which became louder. A faint scream sounded, then another. The tinkle developed into the sound made by breaking glass, and the scraping sound became that of the broken fragments as they rubbed against the sides of the tower in their fall.

The scream came again. It was the frightened cry of a woman. A soft body struck the earth not ten feet from where Arthur stood, then another, and another.

XI

Arthur urged the elevator boy to greater speed. They were speeding up the shaft as rapidly as possible, but it was not fast enough. When they at last reached the height at which the excitement seemed to be centered, the car was stopped with a jerk and Arthur dashed down the hall.

Half a dozen frightened stenographers stood there, huddled together.

"What's the matter?" Arthur demanded. Men were running, from the other floors to see what the trouble was.

"The—the windows broke, and—and something flew in at us!" one of them gasped. There was a crash inside the nearest office and the women screamed again.

Arthur drew a revolver from his pocket and advanced to the door. He quickly threw it open, entered, and closed it behind him. Those left out in the hall waited tensely.

There was no sound. The women began to look even more frightened. The men shuffled their feet uneasily, and looked uncomfortably at one another. Van Deventer appeared on the scene, puffing a little from his haste.

The door opened again and Arthur came out. He was carrying something in his hands. He had put his revolver aside and looked somewhat foolish but very much delighted.

"The food question is settled," he said happily. "Look!"

He held out the object he carried. It was a bird, apparently a pigeon of some sort. It seemed to have been stunned, but as Arthur held it out it stirred, then struggled, and in a moment was flapping wildly in an attempt to escape.

THE RUNAWAY SKYSCRAPER

"It's a wood-pigeon," said Arthur. "They must fly after dark sometimes. A big flock of them ran afoul of the tower and were dazed by the lights. They've broken a lot of windows, I dare say, but a great many of them ran into the stonework and were stunned. I was outside the tower, and when I came in they were dropping to the ground by hundreds. I didn't know what they were then, but if we wait twenty minutes or so I think we can go out and gather up our supper and breakfast and several other meals, all at once."

Estelle had appeared and now reached out her hands for the bird.

"I'll take care of this one," she said. "Wouldn't it be a good idea to see if there aren't some more stunned in the other offices?"

*

In half an hour the electric stoves of the restaurant were going at their full capacity. Men, cheerfully excited men now, were bringing in pigeons by armfuls, and other men were skinning them. There was no time to pluck them, though a great many of the women were busily engaged in that occupation.

As fast as the birds could be cooked they were served out to the impatient but much cheered castaways, and in a little while nearly every person in the place was walking casually about the halls with a roasted, broiled, or fried pigeon in his hands. The ovens were roasting pigeons, the frying-pans were frying them, and the broilers were loaded down with the small but tender birds.

The unexpected solution of the most pressing question cheered every one amazingly. Many people were still frightened, but less frightened than before. Worry for their families still oppressed a great many, but the removal of the fear of immediate hunger led them to believe that the other problems before them would be solved, too, and in as satisfactory a manner.

Arthur had returned to his office with four broiled pigeons in a sheet of wrapping-paper. As he somehow expected, Estelle was waiting there.

"Thought I'd bring lunch up," he announced. "Are you hungry?"

"Starving!" Estelle replied, and laughed.

The whole catastrophe began to become an adventure. She bit eagerly into a bird. Arthur began as hungrily on another. For some time neither spoke a word. At last, however, Arthur waved the leg of his second pigeon toward his desk.

"Look what we've got here!" he said.

Estelle nodded. The stunned pigeon Arthur had first picked up was tied by one foot to a paper-weight.

"I thought we might keep him for a souvenir," she suggested.

"You seem pretty confident we'll get back, all right," Arthur observed. "It was surely lucky those blessed birds came along. They've heartened up the people wonderfully!"

"Oh, I knew you'd manage somehow!" said Estelle confidently.

"I manage?" Arthur repeated, smiling. "What have I done?"

"Why, you've done everything," affirmed Estelle stoutly. "You've told the people what to do from the very first, and you're going to get us back."

Arthur grinned, then suddenly his face grew a little more serious.

"I wish I were as sure as you are," he said. "I think we'll be all right, though, sooner or later."

"I'm sure of it," Estelle declared with conviction. "Why, you—"

"Why I?" asked Arthur again. He bent forward in his chair and fixed his eyes on Estelle's. She looked up, met his gaze, and stammered.

"You—you do things," she finished lamely.

"I'm tempted to do something now," Arthur said. "Look here, Miss Woodward, you've been in my employ for three or four months. In all that time I've never had anything but the most impersonal comments from you. Why the sudden change?"

The twinkle in his eyes robbed his words of any impertinence.

"Why, I really—I really suppose I never noticed you before," said Estelle.

"Please notice me hereafter," said Arthur. "I have been noticing you. I've been doing practically nothing else."

Estelle flushed again. She tried to meet Arthur's eyes and failed. She bit desperately into her pigeon drumstick, trying to think of something to say.

"When we get back," went on Arthur meditatively, "I'll have nothing to do—no work or anything. I'll be broke and out of a job."

Estelle shook her head emphatically. Arthur paid no attention.

"Estelle," he said, smiling, "would you like to be out of a job with me?"

Estelle turned crimson.

"I'm not very successful," Arthur went on soberly. "I'm afraid I wouldn't make a very good husband, I'm rather worthless and lazy!"

"You aren't," broke in Estelle; "you're—you're—"

Arthur reached over and took her by the shoulders.

"What?" he demanded.

She would not look at him, but she did not draw away. He held her from him for a moment.

"What am I?" he demanded again. Somehow he found himself kissing the tips of her ears. Her face was buried against his shoulder.

"What am I?" he repeated sternly.

Her voice was muffled by his coat.

"You're—you're dear!" she said.

There was an interlude of about a minute and a half, then she pushed him away from her.

"Don't!" she said breathlessly. "Please don't!"

"Aren't you going to marry me?" he demanded.

Still crimson, she nodded shyly. He kissed her again.

"Please don't!" she protested.

She fondled the lapels of his coat, quite content to have his arms about her.

"Why mayn't I kiss you if you're going to marry me?" Arthur demanded.

She looked up at him with an air of demure primness.

"You—you've been eating pigeon," she told him in mock gravity, "and—and your mouth is greasy!"

XII

It was two weeks later. Estelle looked out over the now familiar wild landscape. It was much the same when she looked far away, but near by there were great changes.

A cleared trail led through the woods to the waterfront, and a raft of logs extended out into the river for hundreds of feet. Both sides of the raft were lined with busy fishermen—men and women, too. A little to the north of the base of the building a huge mound of earth smoked sullenly. The coal in the cellar had given out and charcoal had been found to be the best substitute they could improvise. The mound was where the charcoal was made.

It was heart-breaking work to keep the fires going with charcoal, because it burned so rapidly in the powerful draft of the furnaces, but the original fire-room gang had been recruited to several times its original number from among the towerites, and the work was divided until it did not seem hard.

As Estelle looked down two tiny figures sauntered across the clearing from the woods with a heavy animal slung between them. One of them was using a gun as a walking-stick. Estelle saw the flash of the sun on its polished metal barrel.

There were a number of Indians in the clearing, watching with wide-open eyes the activities of the whites. Dozens of birch-bark canoes dotted the Hudson, each with its load of fishermen, industriously working for the white people. It had been hard to overcome the fear in the Indians, and they still paid superstitious reverence to the whites, but fair dealings, coupled with a constant readiness to defend themselves, had enabled Arthur to institute a system of trading for food that had so far proved satisfactory.

The whites had found spare electric-light bulbs valuable currency in dealing with the redmen. Picture-wire, too, was highly prized. There was not a picture left hanging in any of the offices. Metal paper-knives bought huge quantities of provisions from the eager Indian traders, and the story was current in the tower that Arthur had received eight canoe-loads of corn and vegetables in exchange for a broken-down typewriter. No one could guess what the savages wanted with the typewriter, but they had carted it away triumphantly.

Estelle smiled tenderly to herself as she remembered how Arthur had been the leading spirit in all the numberless enterprises in which the castaways had been forced to engage. He would come to her in a spare ten minutes, and tell her how everything was going. He seemed curiously boylike in those moments.

Sometimes he would come straight from the fire-room—he insisted on taking part in all the more arduous duties—having hastily cleaned himself for her inspection, snatch a hurried kiss, and then go off, laughing, to help chop down trees for the long fishing-raft. He had told them how to make charcoal, had taken a leading part in establishing and maintaining friendly relations with the Indians, and was now down in the deepest sub-basement, working with a gang of volunteers to try to put the building back where it belonged.

Estelle had said, after the collapse of the flooring in the board-room, that she heard a sound like the rushing of waters. Arthur, on examining the floor where the safe-deposit vault stood, found it had risen an inch. On these facts he had built up his theory. The building, like all modern sky-scrapers, rested on concrete piles extending down to bedrock. In the center of one of those piles there was a hollow tube originally intended to serve as an artesian well. The flow had been insufficient and the well had been stopped up.

THE RUNAWAY SKYSCRAPER

Arthur, of course, as an engineer, had studied the construction of the building with great care, and happened to remember that this partly hollow pile was the one nearest the safe-deposit vault. The collapse of the board-room floor had suggested that some change had happened in the building itself, and that was found when he saw that the deposit-vault had actually risen an inch.

He at once connected the rise in the flooring above the hollow pile with the pipe in the pile. Estelle had heard liquid sounds. Evidently water had been forced into the hollow artesian pipe under an unthinkable pressure when the catastrophe occurred.

From the rumbling and the suddenness of the whole catastrophe a volcanic or seismic disturbance was evident. The connection of volcanic or seismic action with a flow of water suggested a geyser or a hot spring of some sort, probably a spring which had broken through its normal confines some time before, but whose pressure had been sufficient to prevent the accident until the failure of its flow.

When the flow ceased the building sank rapidly. For the fact that this "sinking" was in the fourth direction—the Fourth Dimension—Arthur had no explanation. He simply knew that in some mysterious way an outlet for the pressure had developed in that fashion, and that the tower had followed the spring in its fall through time.

The sole apparent change in the building had occurred above the one hollow concrete pile, which seemed to indicate that if access were to be had to the mysterious, and so far only assumed spring, it must be through that pile. While the vault retained its abnormal elevation, Arthur believed that there was still water at an immense and incalculable pressure in the pipe. He dared not attempt to tap the pipe until the pressure had abated.

At the end of a week he found the vault slowly settling back into place. When its return to the normal was complete he dared begin boring a hole to reach the hollow tube in the concrete pile.

As he suspected, he found water in the pile—water whose sulfurous and mineral nature confirmed his belief that a geyser reaching deep into the bosom of the earth, as well as far back in the realms of time, was at the bottom of the extraordinary jaunt of the tower.

Geysers were still far from satisfactory things to explain. There are many of their vagaries which we cannot understand at all. We do know a few things which affect them, and one thing is that "soaping" them will stimulate their flow in an extraordinary manner.

Arthur proposed to "soap" this mysterious geyser when the renewal of its flow should lift the runaway sky-scraper back to the epoch from which the failure of the flow had caused it to fall.

He made his preparations with great care. He confidently expected his plan to work, and to see the sky-scraper once more towering over mid-town New York as was its wont, but he did not allow the fishermen and hunters to relax their efforts on that account. They labored as before, while deep down in the sub-basement of the colossal building Arthur and his volunteers toiled mightily.

They had to bore through the concrete pile until they reached the hollow within it. Then, when the evidence gained from the water in the pipe had confirmed his surmises, they had to prepare their "charge" of soapy liquids by which the geyser was to be stirred to renewed activity.

Great quantities of the soap used by the scrubwomen in scrubbing down the floors was boiled with water until a sirupy mess was evolved. Means had then to be provided by which this could be quickly introduced into the hollow pile, the hole then closed, and then braced to withstand a pressure unparalleled in hydraulic science.

THE RUNAWAY SKYSCRAPER

Arthur believed that from the hollow pile the soapy liquid would find its way to the geyser proper, where it would take effect in stimulating the lessened flow to its former proportions. When that took place he believed that the building would return as swiftly and as surely as it had left them to normal, modern times.

The telephone rang in his office, and Estelle answered it. Arthur was on the wire. A signal was being hung out for all the castaway to return to the building from their several occupations. They were about to soap the geyser.

Did Estelle want to come down and watch? She did! She stood in the main hallway as the excited and hopeful people trooped in. When the last was inside the doors were firmly closed. The few friendly Indians outside stared perplexedly at the mysterious white strangers.

The whites, laughing excitedly, began to wave to the Indians. Their leave-taking was premature.

Estelle took her way down into the cellar. Arthur was awaiting her arrival. Van Deventer stood near, with the grinning, grimy members of Arthur's volunteer work gang. The massive concrete pile stood in the center of the cellar. A big steam-boiler was coupled to a tiny pipe that led into the heart of the mass of concrete. Arthur was going to force the soapy liquid into the hollow pile by steam.

At a signal steam began to hiss in the boiler. Live steam from the fire-room forced the soapy sirup out of the boiler, through the small iron pipe, into the hollow that led to the geyser far underground. Six thousand gallons in all were forced into the opening in a space of three minutes.

Arthur's grimy gang began to work with desperate haste. Quickly they withdrew the iron pipe and inserted a long steel plug, painfully beaten from a bar of solid metal. Then, girding the colossal concrete pile, ring after ring of metal was slipped on, to hold the plug in place.

The last of the safeguards was hardly fastened firmly when Estelle listened intently.

"I hear a rumbling!" she said quietly.

Arthur reached forward and put his hand on the mass of concrete.

"It is quivering!" he reported as quietly. "I think we'll be on our way in a very little while."

The group broke for the stairs, to watch the panorama as the runaway sky-scraper made its way back through the thousands of years to the times that had built it for a monument to modern commerce.

Arthur and Estelle went high up in the tower. From the window of Arthur's office they looked eagerly, and felt the slight quiver as the tower got under way. Estelle looked up at the sun, and saw it mend its pace toward the west.

Night fell. The evening sounds became high-pitched and shrill, then seemed to cease altogether.

In a very little while there was light again, and the sun was speeding across the sky. It sank hastily, and returned almost immediately, *via* the east. Its pace became a breakneck rush. Down behind the hills and up in the east. Down in the west, up in the east. Down and up— The flickering began. The race back toward modern times had started.

Arthur and Estelle stood at the window and looked out as the sun rushed more and more rapidly across the sky until it became but a streak of light, shifting first to the right and then to the left as the seasons passed in their turn.

With Arthur's arms about her shoulders, Estelle stared out across the unbelievable landscape, while the nights and days, the winters and summers, and the storms and calms of a thousand years swept past them into the irrevocable past.

Presently Arthur drew her to him and kissed her. While he kissed her, so swiftly did the days and years flee by, three generations were born, grew and begot children, and died again!

Estelle, held fast in Arthur's arms, thought nothing of such trivial things. She put her arms about his neck and kissed him, while the years passed them unheeded.

*

Of course you know that the building landed safely, in the exact hour, minute, and second from which it started, so that when the frightened and excited people poured out of it to stand in Madison Square and feel that the world was once more right side up, their hilarious and incomprehensible conduct made such of the world as was passing by think a contagious madness had broken out.

Days passed before the story of the two thousand was believed, but at last it was accepted as truth, and eminent scientists studied the matter exhaustively.

There has been one rather queer result of the journey of the runaway sky-scraper. A certain Isidore Eckstein, a dealer in jewelry novelties, whose office was in the tower when it disappeared into the past, has entered suit in the courts of the United States against all the holders of land on Manhattan Island. It seems that during the two weeks in which the tower rested in the wilderness he traded independently with one of the Indian chiefs, and in exchange for two near-pearl necklaces, sixteen finger-rings, and one dollar in money, received a title-deed to the entire island.—He claims that his deed is a conveyance made previous to all other sales whatever.

Strictly speaking, he is undoubtedly right, as his deed was signed before the discovery of America. The courts, however, are deliberating the question with a great deal of perplexity.

Eckstein is quite confident that in the end his claim will be allowed and he will be admitted as the sole owner of real-estate on Manhattan Island, with all occupiers of buildings and territory paying him ground rent at a rate he will fix himself. In the mean time, though the foundations are being reinforced so the catastrophe cannot occur again, his entire office is packed full of articles suitable for trading with the Indians. If the tower makes another trip back through time, Eckstein hopes to become a landholder of some importance.

No less than eighty-seven books have been written by members of the memorable two thousand in description of their trip to the hinterland of time, but Arthur, who could write more intelligently about the matter than any one else, is so extremely busy that he cannot bother with such things. He has two very important matters to look after. One is, of course, the reenforcement of the foundations of the building so that a repetition of the catastrophe cannot occur, and the other is to convince his wife—who is Estelle, naturally—that she is the most adorable person in the universe. He finds the latter task the more difficult, because she insists that *he* is the most adorable person—